THE LADY'S WAGER

SURRENDERED HEARTS - BOOK TWO

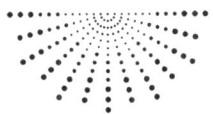

ROSIE CHAPEL

First printing 2018

ISBN: 978-0-6488365-1-3 (e-book)
ISBN: 978-0-6451116-6-8 (paperback)

Ulfire Pty. Ltd.
P.O. Box 1481
South Perth
WA 6951
Australia

www.rosiechapel.com

Front Cover designed by Lisa Miller with Got You Covered
Reverse Cover designed by Rosie Chapel
Images courtesy Period Images and Deposit Photos

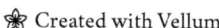 Created with Vellum

ACKNOWLEDGMENTS

Heartfelt thanks to YM Zachary and JB Jospeh for inviting me to contribute to the anthology in which this was originally published. I am honoured.
Grateful thanks to my very supportive friends and family.
Thank you to Lisa Miller with Got You Covered, for this beautiful cover!

For those who show courage and determination
in the face of seemingly insurmountable odds,
This book is dedicated to you

The Lady's Wager
Surrendered Hearts ~ Book 2

A Regency Novelette

CHAPTER ONE

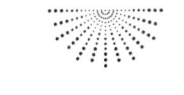

SEPTEMBER 1819

"*P*lease tell me this will be over soon," Gerard Mowbray groused to Randolph Craythorpe, his best friend, and sometime associate in the game of shadows they played for King and Country.

"What is your problem, Ged? 'Tis a wedding, try to enjoy yourself."

"Yes, and thereby hangs another tale. What on earth did Nate want to marry *that* bluestocking for? He could do so much better. I give it less than a year." Ged grumbled.

"The devil, Ged! Nate and Juli are hopelessly in love. If you cannot see that, you need spectacles or, at the very least, a quizzing glass." Randolph glared at his friend in exasperation.

Ever since Nathaniel Livingston, the last of their trio, met Juliette St Clair, Ged had done nothing but moan and complain, believing Juliette would come between them, and spoil their friendship.

It was early September, and the pair were sitting in a quiet corner of the ballroom at Radclyffe Hall, the St Clair's country estate. The day, warm for the time of year, saw most of the guests wandering the sunny gardens or sipping fruit punch in the salon.

Tables, laden with tasty treats were scattered throughout the rooms, and along the two wide terraces. A few couples circled the dance floor to the strains of Mozart, Hayden or Beethoven.

Sounds of laughter and happy chatter wafted through the French doors standing open to allow the balmy air to drift through — the atmosphere, convivial.

The ceremony itself was dignified and, to Randolph and Ged's relief, short. The festivities began immediately thereafter with a traditional wedding breakfast.

Lavish servings of ham and tongue, with perfectly cooked eggs on the side. Pieces of delicately poached fish or white soup for those who preferred something lighter, topped off with fresh bread rolls and hot buttered toast. Hot chocolate to drink, and taking pride of place in the centre of the table was the wedding cake.

An afternoon of leisurely entertainment followed. Juliette and Nathaniel had requested this be an informal gathering, more akin to a garden party than a wedding. A decision received by Society with curiosity — and no small hint of sarcasm, Juliette's quirks well-known — turned to delight at the relaxed ambience of the day.

Randolph considered the matter at hand. Had Ged's pique occurred fifteen, even ten, years ago when they were callow youths, Randolph might be more sympathetic, but they were nearing thirty, far too old to believe a woman was capable of spoiling a friendship, steadfast since all were children.

Juliette's presence merely altered her new husband's priorities. The three saw each other as frequently as they had before Nathaniel met Juliette, and all continued to be involved in the same covert operations.

It was as though Ged did not want to grow up, to assume the mantle of adulthood. To him, their work, while serious and often dangerous, was more an adventure, just one for which he got paid.

The second son of a viscount, it was unlikely the constraints of the title would ever fall on him; Ged's older brother had an heir, and their father was the picture of health. Thus Ged remained content, unravelling whatever mystery their boss, Lucas Withers, set them.

To Ged, women were useful for one thing, and that was *not* a topic for genteel conversation.

Randolph sighed. Of late, he also found his heart touched by another, not that he was prepared to apprise Ged. Felicity Hartwich, a young lady he met at a recent ball. It was early days, all they had shared was the odd smile, a snatch of conversation, and as many dances as he could persuade her into. Her face floated into his mind.

Felicity was not classically beautiful, but she had a wonderful smile, and her hair shone in the candlelight, or the sunlight, or the moonlight…! Catching himself before he lost concentration completely, Randolph dragged his attention back to Ged.

"Why do you not ask a lady to dance? Women usually throw themselves at you, although why eludes me, you treat them with nothing but scorn, but mayhap a dance or two will cheer you up."

"Only one thing will cheer me up and that's more whisky," muttered Ged. Then, realising how petulant he sounded, pulled himself together. "Beg pardon, Randi. Ignore me. I know I am morose. Now Nathaniel is leg-shackled, Father thinks it's time *I* wed."

He shuddered at the very idea. "He and Mama keep introducing me to *suitable prospects*," he sneered the words. "I may have to flee the country." This last said contemplatively.

Randolph barked with laughter at his friend's expression. "Stop being so dramatic, Ged. I'll wager, before six months are up, you *will* be wed."

Ged gaped at him in horror. "Randolph Craythorpe, and you consider yourself my friend? How dare you suggest such a thing? If we were not at a wedding, I might call you out, instead I counter your wager. What are the terms?"

Randolph mused for a moment, then, "White's subscription and a dozen bottles of whisky. Not too onerous." Grinning wickedly, knowing how Ged hated handing over spirits.

"Well, prepare to hand over your coin and your liquor, my good man, because I will *never* marry."

CHAPTER TWO

*W*ithin earshot of this conversation, a young woman, whose family wanted her to marry a second cousin — a man with the personality of a dead tree branch — pondered Ged's words. She knew Gerard Mowbray.

The two had grown up together, both belonging to a large, close-knit group of children whose fathers knew or were related to each other.

Now as adults, their paths crossed occasionally at Society events. Any interaction was usually limited to their somewhat acerbic debates over the latest scandal, political or otherwise, but despite an outward antipathy, Ged and she seemed to empathise with one another, maybe recognising a kindred spirit.

Not that either admitted it, of course.

She tapped her chin, an idea beginning to simmer, one which might win one his bet and give another her freedom, if only briefly.

❧

Melissa Bouchard knew the only reason anyone would agree to marry her was because of her dowry. It was huge. Her father, third Earl of Shepparton, had inherited vast sums, married a woman of similar wealth, and over the years had been canny with it, accumulating an enviable fortune.

Matilda, her adored twin, would win in the marriage stakes. She was the epitome of elegant refinement; never a hair out of place, her gowns pristine, and her accomplishments lauded.

Melissa on the other hand, hated the limelight, and avoided it whenever possible. If she absolutely could not get out of a ball or soiree, she clung to the periphery. It was easier to lurk there than face the snide comments, and pitying glances from her peers, and their mothers.

Born with a damaged foot and, as though that was not bad enough, an ugly birthmark marred a complexion otherwise flawless. As a child, Melissa was unable to join in the riotous games loved by her playmates, and instead spent her days hunched over a book, or lost in daydreams.

An avid reader, she had devoured every tome in her father's library, twice, then begged her friends to grant access to their collections. Had she allowed her misfortune to rule her, Melissa's childhood might have been lonely, but if she had a book, she was never alone.

Tall, with raven hair and eyes as green as emeralds, at first glance, Melissa was the more vibrant version of the sisters — her twin's colouring being softer, paler — but people rarely noticed.

What they *did* notice was her sturdy cane, her awkward gait, and the smudge, which ran in angry purple from the lobe of her right ear, across the edge of her check and half way down her neck.

Clever hairstyles and powder hid the worst of it, but Melissa was not naive, her dowry was the attraction, not her. In a world where unblemished beauty was like gold, Melissa Bouchard was considered less than brass.

Refusing to let her impediment define her, neither would Melissa be cowed or ruled. Upon reaching her majority, she had informed her parents she intended to remain a spinster rather than marry a man who cared only for her inheritance, standing firm in the face of her parents' ambitions.

Matilda, or Mattie as everyone called her, was Melissa's staunchest ally. The two were closer than most sisters, but Mattie was being courted by the son of a duke and, already, there were whispers of a proposal in the not too distant future.

Thus, she was rarely at home to act as a buffer between her mother and her twin. The distinct possibility of such a high status marriage meant their Mama ensured Melissa stayed out of the way. No need to scare off a suitor by introducing the ugly sister, which in all honesty, did not bother Melissa one jot; Society gatherings being the bane of her existence.

The only reason Lady Shepparton did not try to prevent her daughter attending this wedding was because Juliette was Melissa's greatest friend, and her absence would be questioned.

Shrugging off a familiar sorrow at what her life might easily become, Melissa let her idea flourish. It could work, if only Ged saw the sense in it

Moments later, Melissa heard Randolph stroll away, whistling a tuneless ditty. Standing, she shook out her gown, seized her courage in both hands and walked to where Ged was sitting.

"Good afternoon, Lord Gerard. It appears, as ever, you are not enjoying yourself. Is it too much to ask that you smile and be glad for your friend? Just this once?"

Ged sprawled on the chair, glowered at the regally tall young woman currently grinning at him. "Lady Melissa," he drawled. "I might guess you would appear just in time to delight in my misery. How do you know the happy couple?"

"Juliette is my best friend."

Ged frowned, realising he already knew that, but he had barely noticed who the guests were — too busy feeling sorry for himself.

"So, Lord Aumale thinks 'tis time you sought a bride? Clearly Nathaniel's nuptials sparked renewed hope you will finally relinquish your rakish lifestyle, and conform to expectations. I wager we could help each other. I, too, find myself being pressed into an alliance for which I have no desire."

Ged's sharp retort froze on his lips when his annoyed gaze collided with Melissa's. Her expression, one of sympathy rather than sarcasm. "Do you often eavesdrop on private conversations?" He could not keep the snide tone out of his voice.

Melissa stared at him until he actually squirmed under her scrutiny. "Goodness, you do have a high opinion of yourself. Why anyone would choose to listen to your whiney gossip is beyond me. No, I was already sitting around the other side of this pillar, minding my own business when you two arrived."

"Yet you opted to stay when you could so easily have moved?"

Melissa flicked a pointed glance to her cane. "Why should I be the one to move?"

This went on for a few minutes, rapidly deteriorating into their habitual mockery, until Melissa, tired of the same old argument, steered the discussion back to the reason she approached him in the first place.

"I did think I might be able to assist you in your endeavours to avoid being married, and win your bet, but I daresay I was mistaken. I realise accepting help from the ungainly wallflower is probably too much, even for you." She paused, her eyes glinting, her hair fairly crackling around her head.

For a split second, Ged was held in thrall by her beauty, a beauty he had no idea she possessed.

Then her lip curled, her tone became caustic, and she was his sparring partner again. "I doubt you will need to worry. Unless the proposed bride is a simpering milksop, your churlish attitude will drive away even the most desperate of ladies. Good day to you."

Despite her best effort, Melissa was unable to hide the flash of hurt in her eyes or the hint of melancholy in her voice.

CHAPTER THREE

*T*ossing her head, Melissa spun around. Her hair, in an intricate coil over her neck, lifted slightly to reveal the hated birthmark.

Gripping her cane, she strode away as quickly as she was able, leaving Ged open-mouthed with astonishment. Melissa never walked away from an argument, she loved them, relished them like the challenge he assumed they were. Was it not to best each other, the reason they began them in the first place?

Unsure now, Ged's brows creased, his eyes drawn to her while she struggled along the edge of the dance floor, head held high, back ramrod straight. A strange emotion settled over him, and he was suddenly intrigued by her scheme.

"Melissa," he called after her, forgetting to use her honorific. Melissa either did not hear or chose to ignore him, for her limping stride did not falter as she disappeared through the glass doors into the long corridor beyond the ballroom.

Melissa was furious with herself. *What on earth possessed her? Why should Ged even listen to her, never mind agree to her plan? She was an idiot. Would she ever learn?*

Despite all evidence to the contrary, Melissa continued to believe most people were innately considerate, unable to accept cruel and thoughtless behaviour was the norm.

Regrettably, of late it was a belief she was finding harder to cling to. She knew Ged cultivated the persona of an incorrigible reprobate, but when they were younger, he was one of a very few who never called her names or laughed at her.

Even now, in the midst of their argument, he did not use her disfigurement as a way to win. She supposed, she ought to be grateful but for some reason his grouchiness stung. Maybe it was because of the happiness of the newlyweds, and the realisation such joy would likely never be hers.

Frustrated with the futility of it all, she heard Ged call her name but pretended she had not, unable to stomach any more negativity — not today.

Hoping no one would see, and encourage her to re-join the festivities, Melissa slipped into the cool of the library. She needed the solace of books, and headed to her favourite section.

Growing up, she had often stayed with Juliette at the Radclyffe's estate, and knew exactly which books were where. Making a beeline for the ancient collection, she found what she sought, a battered copy of Virgil's Aeneid.

Her fingers caressed the volume as she lifted it down, and sinking into one of the leather chairs by the open French window, she inhaled the aroma of the faded pages.

Bliss.

Nestling into the seat and enjoying the balmy breeze, she

opened the book, immediately losing herself in a world of love, loss and betrayal.

§❧

Unbeknownst to Melissa, Ged had tracked her progress, following her into the library, where he paused, silent and motionless, half-hidden by the door, watching her remove the book from the shelf.

The way her slender fingers stroked the tome sent unexpected heat along his veins and he was beset by an overwhelming urge to discover what lay beneath her impenetrable façade.

Was it worth listening to her... wager?

A wry grin tugged at the corners of his mouth at her audacity. The Melissa he knew was cautious, weighing up everything before she spoke, as their many disagreements attested.

She never made a sweeping statement, everything she discussed, she supported with some kind of evidence. If she had a plan, it would be meticulously considered. Mayhap he should give her a chance.

Engrossed in the story, Melissa did not hear Ged's footfall on the thick rug, giving him a moment to observe her unnoticed. Unbidden, he recalled carefree days of childhood, when he refused to let her hide, inventing games which did not involve running about so she could participate. Her disability had never been an issue for him; in truth he barely noticed it.

Bringing his mind back to the present, Ged registered that the afternoon sun through the window caught a sprinkling of interesting red and copper highlights in her inky hair.

The bend of her neck exposed a smooth curve of alabaster skin, and it was all he could to not to reach out and see whether it felt as satiny as it looked.

Her fingers rested on the pages of the book, and she had curled her legs underneath her, skirts covering her shoes.

That same elusive emotion rippled through Ged, and he paused. For one usually so confidant, he was disconcerted. This was unlike him; he cared little for the sensitivities of others, women especially.

He found them clingy, annoying and far too interested in their looks or the latest fashions. They served one purpose, and that thirst could be quenched without the necessity for a binding, lifelong contract.

So what was it about Melissa?

He cleared his throat, causing the subject of his musings to squawk in shock.

"The devil, Ged Mowbray," she snapped, reverting to familiarity without thinking. "What on earth are you doing, sneaking up on a person? Do you wish to give me apoplexy?" Melissa swivelled in her seat to glare at him suspiciously.

Ged opened his palms in a gesture of contrition. "My apologies, Lady Melissa. I had no mind to give you a fright," he paused, swallowing, in a bid to control the rush of blood to his loins prompted by the fire in her astonishingly green eyes. Forcing the confusion of thoughts from his head, he continued, "I wondered whether you might care to elaborate?"

"On what?" she demanded sharply.

"Your wager."

CHAPTER FOUR

*M*elissa gaped. *What,* now *he wanted to listen?* She stared at Ged, registering, possibly for the first time, how handsome he had become.

When they were younger, she considered him a gangling youth — too tall and too thin, his hair too long. Studying him dispassionately, she realised, if she stood, he would tower above her, and she was tall for a woman, but he was broader now, a physique honed and taut.

An odd quiver ran through her.

Slowly, and with absolutely no awareness of what her scrutiny was doing to Ged, she ran her eyes over him, noticing the muscles flexing under his dark blue coat when he shifted his stance and folded his arms.

She craned her neck, the better to see his face; clean shaven, angular cheekbones under rich brown eyes, framed by dark lashes. Forgetting he was waiting for her to speak, she let her gaze travel to his thick auburn hair trimmed short, but with an endearing scruffiness to it.

Endearing? Heavens, Melissa, she chastised, *feet back on the ground, girl.*

. . .

As though uncomfortable under her perceptive regard, Ged coughed, bringing Melissa's eyes to his. Shaking her head, she muttered something unintelligible, and made to stand.

"Let us remain seated, I imagine this discussion might take a while." Ged suggested. Gratefully, Melissa acquiesced; unwilling to confess she found standing for any length of time, arduous. Ged took the seat facing hers, at the other side of the French door and they sat in silence for several minutes.

How to broach this topic? Melissa deliberated for a moment, then gave up trying to marshal her thoughts and simply launched in.

"Lord Gerard." She noticed Ged raise an eyebrow. "Well, I cannot call you Ged, it would be presumptuous, and Mowbray sounds as though I am addressing your father. No, no, Lord Gerard it must be. Stop distracting me," she scolded lightly.

He grinned at her expression, and suddenly the tension between them lightened.

"Where was I? Yes. Let me see… your parents are trying to marry you off. Your friend thinks you will be wed before six months are out. You do not want to marry." Melissa ticked them off on one hand as she listed them, and then looked him dead in the eye. "Am I correct thus far?"

Ged nodded.

"My parents are also determined to find me a spouse, willing or not," she bit her lip. "I have no desire to marry unless 'tis for love, and I am not foolish enough to believe that is ever going to happen."

Her no nonsense tones in stark contrast with the unutterable sadness flickering across her face, gone so quickly, Ged was not certain he saw it.

"I wish to travel. Around this England, should that be all I am able to manage, but the continent is my preference. To see Rome, and Greece. To visit sites of antiquity. To see where my heroes lived."

She stopped, such dreams were not meant to be shared. They would be ridiculed, for how could a cripple walk through ruins? She dipped her head, biting her lip to prevent more rubbish from spilling out of her mouth, or the tears, which threatened. She was stronger than this. Sucking in a deep breath, she blinked furiously, and raised her head, surprising a curious expression on Ged's face.

While she talked, Ged tried to concentrate, this was why he followed her to the library, but his eyes continually strayed to her bottom lip, currently clamped between pearly white teeth. He wanted to rub his thumb over the abused skin, no — what he actually wanted to do was kiss it.

Wait ... what...? Kiss Melissa? No, no, no, absolutely not. It was the whisky, muddling his brain. The whisky, the sunshine and Randi's stupid wager. He forced his attention back to what Melissa was saying

"...if you do not think it too awful to spend the next few months pretending to court me, we both win."

Court her? Damn it all, what did he miss?

"Err ... I beg your pardon, might you repeat that last part, to ensure there is no misunderstanding?"

Melissa pinned him with a steely look, the green of her eyes darkening. Huffing a sigh, she repeated.

"If it appears we have developed an affection, a *tendre*, and were you to escort me to balls, soirees, the theatre and so on, our parents might believe it to be serious. At the end of the six months, we can have a fight or I can be appalled at you having a mistress, or frequenting brothels or gaming hells, or some such thing, and break it off. You are not married, I am not married. You win the bet. Your parents, sympathetic to your distress, will leave you alone."

"Perhaps you do not understand the terms of a wager. There is a winner and a loser."

"Oh, I am happy to be the loser. You win your bet with Lord Randolph. Your parents stop pestering you to marry. Mine, on the other hand, will be terribly upset…" she flicked open her fan, wafting it in the agitated manner so adored by discomposed mamas, the gesture drawing a chuckle from Ged, "…with no alternative but to send me to the continent to escape the ensuing scandal." Smiling at him, mischief in her eyes.

"You wish to visit Europe so badly you would risk your reputation?" Ged queried, his mind turning her idea over and over. There was no downside, ignoring the peculiar ache in the region of his heart, at Melissa's willingness to take the blame, so she could run away.

It was a tantalising plan and in the guise of ruminating over it, he took the opportunity to study her again. So, she had a birthmark? It was not too obvious, admiring the lustrous black swathe of hair falling in one heavy coil over her shoulder, veiling the blemish.

His gaze swept across her throat, to the delicate neckline of her pale green gown, which now he looked more closely, seemed to shimmer when she moved. Unlike many of her peers, Melissa was not willowy thin, but in no way could she be described as plump. Ged decided 'shapely' to be the best description, imagining his fingers tracing her figure.

He gulped. *This had to stop.*

CHAPTER FIVE

"*W*hat do you think? Might you be able to suffer my company for a few months, to give us both a little freedom, a little peace?" Melissa whispered, the wait agonising. "I know 'tis unconventional, and I understand if you deem it too high a price."

All at once, the idea, which seemed the answer to her prayers, sounded juvenile and crass. She hastened to spare him from rejecting her suggestion outright.

"Forget it, Ged. Forget I ever spoke to you of this. I did not think it through. No one would believe you are interested in courting me, they would think you were settling for second best because Mattie has a suitor, or you were after my dowry. You would be subject to mean-spirited gossips the whole time and I do not wish that for you, definitely not you." Melissa's voice dropped to a murmur, and she saw no reason to clarify her last words.

Unfolding her legs from under her, she reached for her cane. Her bad foot was numb, obliging her to flex it in the tight shoe until the circulation returned. Tutting in frustration, Melissa shifted her weight to her good foot, standing on the rug carefully, using the cane for balance.

Smoothing her skirts, she continued. "My apologies, Lord Gerard. Thank you for taking the time to listen to my ridiculous scheme. Mayhap we shall meet again soon," her tone giving every indication she would avoid him like the plague.

She walked unsteadily to the French doors, intent on getting as far away from this man as possible. This man who, in the space of an hour, had gone from annoying friend — was he ever a friend?

Maybe when they were children, now close acquaintance was a better description — to a man she wanted to kiss, to touch, to stroke his skin. Her cheeks flared with hectic colour. *Gracious, she was nothing short of wanton.*

An image of him naked popped into her mind, and a soft whimper fluttered over her lips. She paused, straightened her shoulders, and limped outside, into the waning afternoon sunshine.

Ged was flummoxed. *What just happened?* One minute she was offering him the chance to beat Randi, and also get his parents off his back, but the next, before he had the chance to say, yay or nay, she yanked it from him. He strode after her, catching her by the elbow as she reached the edge of the terrace.

"Mel… Lady Melissa, wait."

She stared pointedly at the hand gripping her arm, until he released it, before lifting her eyes to his.

Ged searched her face, reading doubt, fear, distress and frustration, all of which he wanted to assuage. "I want in." He held her gaze steadily, observing a flicker of something in their fathomless green depths.

Was it hope? Relief? He liked to think it was one or both.

Not one for subtle nuances or guileful innuendo, Ged perceived there were complexities to Melissa, and for no reason he could think of, he wanted to unravel all of them.

He did not understand why, or what prompted it but, out of the blue, to spend six months with this young woman was something he definitely did not want to miss.

❦

The next few weeks were surreal for Melissa.

The instant Ged agreed to her proposal, he assumed control. Careful to let their relationship appear to be developing gradually, he invited her for carriage rides, or would happen upon her at a picnic both attended. Once he even contrived to meet her at the museum, astonishing her with his knowledge of the Elgin Marbles in the Greek exhibit.

Lady Shepparton, Melissa's mother, fawned all over him, to Melissa's mortification, and her father put him on the spot the first time he came calling. Ged behaved impeccably and, to outward appearances, seemed enamoured with their daughter.

Melissa in her turn, comported herself in the manner expected from a well-brought up young lady of the *ton*, politely and with grace. She was beginning to chafe though. They never did anything exciting.

She could go to picnics or take carriage rides any time. She wanted to be daring, to take a risk and, unexpectedly, the more she came to know him, the more she really, *really* wanted Ged to kiss her. It might be the only chance she would have.

. . .

They talked for hours, discovering, and in some cases re-discovering, their common interests. Ged made Melissa laugh — a lot, delighting in her irreverent sense of humour. Her refusal to consider her damaged foot a hindrance had always impressed him but now, Ged discovered she had talents of which many were unaware.

As well as her love of books and learning, Melissa was a proficient horsewoman, a gifted artist, and could demolish the opposition at pall mall. The latter being a popular game whereby, using a wooden mallet, the players hit a ball down a long alley and through a loop at the far end. The winner, the one to so in the fewest hits. Melissa was almost always able to get the ball through the loop with one strike.

Without realising it, Ged curbed his wild ways. He still enjoyed a whisky, but less frequently than was his habit. Gaming hells, with accompanying extras, lost their attraction.

Instead, Ged opted to spend evenings with Melissa at the theatre, or simply talking by the fire. Had any of his friends witnessed this abrupt transformation, they would struggle to comprehend it. Ged did not even notice.

They continued to argue, relishing the banter in which they always partook. The subject was irrelevant — politics, the weather, fashion, the latest scandal, which, to their amusement often targeted Melissa anyway — they thrived on it, often playing devil's advocate just to rile the other up.

The longer they spent together the more both realised how much they liked and appreciated each other. What was forged in childhood, matured into mutual affection, hovering on the brink of something else entirely.

Not that either discerned it yet.

CHAPTER SIX

*T*hree months after Juliette's wedding, Ged received an invitation to a weekend house party at Shepparton Manor, deep in the Buckinghamshire countryside, and a day's ride from London.

November was sliding into December, yet even as winter spread its frosty blanket, remnants of glorious autumnal hues hung on, tenacious pockets of red, yellow and bronze. The landscape was breathtaking.

The Bouchard family departed early in the week, Ged confirming he would leave the city on Friday morning, aiming to be at the estate by late afternoon. Mattie's current suitor would also attend, as would a selection of family friends.

Normally, Melissa hated these gatherings, they were just one more instance where hiding in the shadows was preferable to being poked, prodded, and questioned. This time she was thrilled. Maybe, just maybe she might persuade Ged to kiss her. She wasn't above begging if she thought she could inveigle him. It was nearly Christmas, it could be his gift.

· · ·

Where this would happen was the easy part.

Shepparton Manor had a maze. Planted by the original owner two hundred years previously, it was the grandfather of puzzles, and not easy to solve. Guests had been known to wander through it for hours before one or other of the Bouchards took pity and rescued them.

Melissa and Mattie had been tumbling though it with varying degrees of agility since they could walk, and knew every twist and turn. At its centre stood an old folly, hidden from view, and quite, *quite* isolated.

How, might prove more difficult.

Melissa thought a challenge might just liven up the weekend.

Perhaps by moonlight.

To Melissa, the week dragged on interminably. Finally, Friday afternoon arrived but, to Melissa's surprise, Ged did not. Darkness fell, the evening unfolded and, while the other guests enjoyed a veritable feast of delicacies, Melissa pushed food around her plate.

Despite knowing their courtship was a sham, nerves beset her, ruining her appetite. No one questioned his absence, accepting Melissa's rather convoluted explanation it was likely business delayed him.

Prior to appearing in the dining room, and almost giddy with anticipation, Melissa had pampered herself. The ritual of washing her hair and soaking in a bath scented with fragrant oil doing little to loosen the knots in her stomach.

Donning her favourite dress of forest green silk, with her

hair twisted into an intricate style, dark locks shimmering in the candlelight, Melissa hoped Ged would recognise she had made the effort for him.

Now, here she was, among all their friends, alone as usual. Where was Ged? Was he simply delayed or had he decided a weekend in her company exceeded the terms of their wager?

On tenterhooks and, after knocking over a glass of wine, spilling a platter of savoury pastries, seemingly just by looking at them, and tripping over non-existent obstacles, Melissa felt it best to excuse herself. Lady Shepparton tutted in exasperation at her clumsy daughter, but did not object.

Melissa hastened to her bedchamber. Sitting on the edge of her bed, heels rhythmically banging on the wooden base, she tried to banish the fidgets, and ignore the voice in her head insisting Ged was not coming.

Why was she so tightly wound about this? If something prevented him from travelling, or he chose to remain in London, it was not the end of the world. Others might be offended, but their opinion should not matter to either Ged or her — it was not as though they were in love.

Just then, the memory of an interlude — which had been, simultaneously, wonderful and unpleasant — popped into Melissa's head.

A little over a fortnight previously, the couple had attended her cousin's birthday ball. Sometime during the evening, Ged persuaded her into a dance. Despite her panic — how was she supposed to dance with her stupid foot? — he encouraged her, and it was one of the most liberating and exhilarating moments of her life. Their conversation remained as clear in her head as though it happened yesterday.

§

Once he had managed to coax her into a dance, Ged did not allow her excuses to deter him. He simply entwined their fingers and asked whether she trusted him.

She stared at their conjoined hands, his huge one engulfing her slender one, and swallowed on a gulp. It was the first time he had taken her hand. They usually linked arms when walking together.

This was a whole new level of intimacy, and she was nonplussed. Refusing to read anything into it, she plastered on a smile.

"Do I trust you, let me think..." she left it dangling, tapping her chin, watching Ged's expression. Just when she deemed him on the verge of irritation, she capitulated.

"Fine, I trust you, but you cannot make me into a princess. I am the frog, or maybe a crab." She chuckled.

Ged smiled, and led her onto the dance floor. She realised it was waltz and tried to untangle their fingers, to escape. What was he thinking? She could not dance a waltz.

He ignored her consternation, and placed his right hand on her waist, clasping the fingers of her right hand with his left. Then they began to move. Ged's firm grasp braced her, and she scarcely needed to use her bad foot.

They did not circle the floor very smoothly, and their turns were not particularly graceful, but they danced a waltz.

When the music died away, she thanked him and dipped a curtsy. Ged took her hand, kissed her knuckles and drew her upright. Briefly their eyes met, and Melissa was almost certain he wanted to kiss her.

It passed so quickly, she presumed it was her overactive imagi-

nation induced by the magic of the moment, determined not to heed the voice insisting it was because she was not perfect.

Melissa had been elated by her achievement, but when Ged escorted her from the ballroom, they passed a group of guests whose comments continued to rankle, even now, over two weeks later.

"So kind of Lord Gerard to take pity on the poor cripple."

"I cannot think why he wastes his time. Lady Melissa is a testy chit, he would be wise to exchange her for a knife, it would be less barbed."

"He is so good looking, he could have any woman. I cannot imagine what he sees in her. Must be her dowry."

...and on and on, laughing uproariously.

Melissa, used to it, made no attempt to set them straight. Ged however turned to address the gossips. She tried to dissuade him; it was a waste of breath.

"Ged, do not engage, they delight in provoking me. I block it out. They do not know me, they do not know us. Let them have their fun." Her voice hard, and emotionless, she pulled him away.

Ged cupped her face, searching her eyes, maybe glimpsing in them more than she was comfortable with, for he dropped a kiss on her forehead and stalked back to the group.

"The next time I hear anyone refer to Lady Melissa as a cripple, I may have to call them out. You believe yourselves to be of the nobility? I am ashamed to think we belong to the same class." The quiet disgust in his tone prompting red faces, and muttered apologies.

"'Tis not me from whom you should beg forgiveness." His gaze bored into each one. Satisfied he had made his point, he returned to her side.

"You did not need to do that, but thank you. I appreciate your concern."

♪

There, in the quiet of her bedchamber, the scene replayed itself over and over, his words reverberating through her. Recalling the touch of his kiss on her forehead — like a brand, eliciting all manner of unfamiliar sensations, she longed to know whether he would evoke the same response, were he to repeat it... on her lips.

Melissa groaned. No! *Hell and damnation* no! This was not supposed to happen, this was so far outside their agreement as to be preposterous.

Neither could she tell anyone, and Ged would vanish like the morning mist under a hot sun if she mentioned it to him. Nor was she brave enough. He would laugh at her feminine foolishness, and say love was for dreamers.

Problem being, Melissa *was* a dreamer, she had always been a dreamer, it was just buried under a veneer of peppery sarcasm.

Well, naught she could do about it, but the realisation made her more determined than ever to steal that kiss, by fair means or foul.

CHAPTER SEVEN

*R*efusing to let Ged's absence bother her, or maybe in response to it, Melissa grabbed an old woollen shawl, and slipped her feet into warm boots.

Lifting her cane out of its stand, she made her painstaking way down the stairs, spying Williams, their butler, lurking at the edge of the hall.

"Williams, I'm going for a walk. No," when he started to speak, "I do not require company, I think I can walk the grounds of my home without a chaperone."

She smiled, but the old retainer noticed it did not quite reach her eyes. *Odd that, she was bright and cheerful earlier today.* Frowning, he continued with his duties, deciding if she did not return within half an hour, to mention it to Lady Matilda.

For all she rarely visited Shepparton Manor anymore, Melissa remained a favourite among the staff, being unfailingly courteous and respectful. As a child she spent more time with them than her family who judged her impediments an embarrassment, and they continued to keep a watchful eye on her.

Cautiously descending the steps leading to the gardens, Melissa found her thoughts straying to her parents. She supposed they cared in their way, but she did not fit a mould, their criterion of how a daughter ought to behave and, unable to make her conform, avoided her.

It dawned on her, except for Lady Shepparton refusing to listen to the doctors when they said Melissa would never walk, instead, encouraging her daughter to persevere, for which she was indebted, her mother barely tolerated her.

To be fair, their relationship was more amenable since this farce upon which Ged and she had embarked, but that was probably in the hope Melissa would soon become someone else's responsibility.

Melissa could not say her mother was cruel or mean-spirited, more... indifferent. She supposed she wasn't the best daughter, being wayward, independently minded and fractious. Thank goodness Mattie was perfect. Melissa gave a snort of bitter laughter, and hobbled into the night.

Not far away, a rider urged on his horse. Inclement weather slowed his journey, making him appallingly late. For a man who, until recently, cared nothing for women's sensitivities, the mere thought of upsetting Melissa made his chest pinch.

Flying along muddy roads for hours, had given Gerard Mowbray plenty of time to think. To his surprise, these last three months had been agreeable. No, that was not good enough; they were splendid. Melissa and he had talked and laughed, engaged in those entertainments and activities deemed suitable for courting couples, genuinely enjoying each other's company.

While he rode, Ged remembered an evening a couple of

weeks ago, when he had convinced her to dance with him.
The conversation continuing to echo in his head

"You are addled if you think I am ever setting foot on the dance floor. The gossips are already having field day with our supposed courtship. We should not give them any more fodder, and this will make you a laughing stock." Melissa said, swatting him with her fan, her merry laugh, and impish grin sending delicious ribbons of heat coiling through him.

"Do you trust me?" he asked, and without thinking, grasped her fingers. He saw how surprised she was at his gesture. Her cheeks bloomed a becoming pink and he heard her quiet gulp. Well, to be fair, it was the first time he had taken her hand. They usually linked arms when walking together, but he rather liked this new intimacy.

He waited for her reply,

"Do I trust you, let me think..." he watched while she tapped her chin, and felt a frown begin to form, bothered by the notion she might not trust him.

"Fine, I trust you, but you cannot make me into a princess. I am the frog, or maybe a crab." Even though Melissa chuckled her answer, an as yet indefinable sensation ran through Ged at her self-deprecating tone.

Pushing it aside for now, he led her onto the dance floor. A Mozart waltz began to play, and Melissa tried to pull away.

"No," she whispered, horrified, "'tis a waltz. Please, you cannot make me do this."

"Melissa Bouchard, have some faith. Now..." he gathered her close, and they began to move.

He made sure he held her firmly enough she scarcely needed to use her bad foot. Granted, they did not circle the floor as quickly as the other dancers, and their cadence was a trifle jerky, but they danced a waltz.

When the music died away, Melissa dipped a low curtsy. "Thank you, Lord Gerard, you have no idea..." she did not finish her sentence.

Ged took her hand, bowed over it and brushed his lips to her knuckles, bringing her upright. As their eyes met, he was captivated by the glow in hers, quelling an almost irresistible impulse to kiss her into oblivion right there, on the dance floor.

Only the belief she had no romantic interest in him — and, of course, with him it was pure lust... wasn't it? — prevented him.

Approaching his destination, Ged reigned in Ruby, his dapple-grey mare, slowing her to a walk and patting her on the shoulder. *Hell's teeth this was a facer. Was he in love with Melissa?* He did not know what love was, but the idea she would walk out of his life in three months' time was something he did not wish to contemplate.

Was that love?

He believed they had become good friends. He looked forward to, and cherished, the hours they spent together. He preferred her company to that of Randi or Nate, which he knew confounded them, but they had kept their counsel thus far. He admired her fortitude in a world, which shunned the imperfect.

Those aspects of herself Melissa regarded as flaws — to Ged, simply elements of a beautiful whole. He ached for her when she overheard a thoughtless remark, yet even though he knew it stung, she did not ask to be pitied or defended; she rose above their pettiness.

Was it love?

What of the wager? Of both wagers?

What of Melissa?

Did she care for him in the same way? When he kissed her hand at the ball after they danced, when he chastised the group of inconsiderate gossips, he discerned a hint of something in her eyes, something more than enjoyment, more than appreciation of his defending her.

*Was there **any** possibility it was love?*

In the middle of a lonely road, on a freezing winter's night, Ged Mowbray stopped questioning. The answer had been there all along.

"Well, this is a pretty pickle," he remarked to Ruby, who nickered in agreement. The wind was bitter and beginning to strengthen; he needed to get to Shepparton Manor.

Nudging Ruby into a steady canter, Gerard Mowbray rode into his destiny.

CHAPTER EIGHT

*M*eanwhile, Melissa was trudging angrily through the frosty gardens and, without conscious awareness, arrived at the entrance to the maze.

Pausing for several seconds, she pondered the wisdom of walking its paths in the dark, in the cold. She was toasty warm, her shawl thick as a cloak, and the rising moon offered sufficient light by which to navigate the maze — its layout, as familiar as the back of her hand.

Making a decision, Melissa stepped forward.

❧

Across the estate, Ged thundered into the rear courtyard, sliding off Ruby's back, and leading her to the trough by the stables. Groomsmen appeared as if by magic, taking the reins — a rub down, and a loose box with a nosebag of hay in the tired mare's immediate future.

· · ·

"Welcome, Lord Mowbray," an amused voice greeted him. It belonged to Mattie.

"Lady Matilda, what are you doing out in the cold? You will catch your death."

"I was walking past the window in the drawing room and saw you hurtling along the drive." She paused. "Melissa was becoming agitated." Her gaze, a subdued version of her twin's, penetrating and quizzical.

"I must apologise to her, and Lady Shepparton, for my tardiness. Bad weather delayed my departure from London."

"She went for a walk."

Ged gawked at Mattie. "I beg your pardon, Lady Matilda, did you say a walk?"

Mattie shrugged, as though such lunacy was normal. "She was dropping things, and tripping over air, so left the dining room. I was going to find her when Williams told me she went out about half an hour ago."

Do you have any idea where she went," he implored, faintly. The night was frigid. What on earth possessed her?

"I imagine she headed for the maze. 'Tis her favourite refuge when things bother her. I think she finds the challenge soothing."

Ged gave a grim smile; that sounded exactly like Melissa. "Please would you be so kind as to direct me to this maze, and offer a hint as to how I might get through it without becoming hopelessly lost?"

Mattie studied him for a moment. "Before I do, may I ask you something?" She waited until he inclined his head. "Are you toying with her? Is this one of your juvenile games, cooked up with Randi Craythorpe? For I warn you, if you hurt my sister I will make your life a living hell." Her gentle voice, at odds with her fierce expression.

"I assure you I am not toying with her. Our... relationship may have begun under dubious circumstances, the terms of which we both agreed upon. In fact, it was her idea, before you take umbrage. I do not know when it changed, but it has, and is something I must discuss with Melissa."

"Do you love her?" Mattie's question, stark as the landscape.

"I might tell you, after I tell her." Was all he said, giving her the answer she needed.

"Three left then one right, do not change the sequence or you will be wandering in there two days hence." She turned to go inside, then spun on her heel. "I shall inform Mama of your arrival, and where you have gone."

Ged spluttered something about propriety and chaperones.

Mattie waved her hand. "No need to fret. Mama is the least of your worries. Do not, I repeat *do not* mess this up." She hurried into the house, leaving Ged in the middle of the dark, cold courtyard — stupefied.

Melissa had reached the centre of the maze. The folly rose up in front of her, silhouetted against the winter's moon. The sky was crystal clear, millions of stars glistening in its obsidian depths. Melissa, resting on her cane, tilted her head backwards, the better to admire them.

She never grew tired of stargazing and here, they always appeared closer than in the city. Hugging the shawl around her, she stepped into the little stone building.

It was barely more than a supported roof, but offered a modicum of shelter. A hexagonal structure, it sported stone benches between five of the pillars and, in the remaining gap, an entrance of sorts.

In the middle of the flagged floor, an old yet solid wooden chest acted as both table and storage. Unlatching the chest,

Melissa withdrew a blanket and two cushions. She unfolded the blanket along one of the benches, and propped the cushions, one atop the other, against one of the pillars, creating a makeshift upright pillow.

Settling onto the blanket, she stretched out her legs, nestled into the cushions, and let her thoughts roam.

What ought she to do? Continue the pretence? Adept at hiding her feelings, Melissa knew, ultimately, this is what she would do. What other choice did she have? Confess to Ged that she harboured an affection, for him?

He would smile, pat her hand and tell her she was imagining things, and she could not face his pity. She might be tempestuous, plucky, and irascible, and yes barbed, but this was unexpected. This was more than she bargained for. To fall in love was not part of the wager.

No, she would see it through, then say goodbye.

Mayhap Rome, with all its wonders would prove an adequate distraction, ignoring the whisper that nothing would heal a shattered heart, caged before ever it had the chance to soar.

Leaning her head against the chill stone, she forced the stupid, frivolous nonsense out of her mind, and closed her eyes.

CHAPTER NINE

*N*ot far away, Ged was questioning whether there was indeed a mid-point within this blasted maze, or whether the whole thing was a trick designed to send unwanted visitors mad.

He followed Mattie's instructions, dubious as to their veracity. He would not put it past her to provide the wrong ones, to test his mettle.

Just when he thought he was never going to come to the centre, he did. Expecting a small enclosure, Ged was astounded by its proportions. A substantial space, with six openings into the maze — should he drop his kerchief by the one he came though?

What if Mattie was incorrect and Melissa had chosen a different walk? He would struggle to retrace his steps.

Standing for a moment, letting his eyes adjust to the moonlight, Ged studied the folly. At the far side, he detected an oddly shaped pillar.

She was here.

His heart thudded.

Did he dare tell her?

He could not hide it any longer, even if she laughed at him, told him it was his imagination, he needed to take the risk.

He walked around to where Melissa was sitting, approaching cautiously so as not to startle her. Her eyes were closed, and in the ethereal light, her skin was reminiscent of the finest porcelain, sooty lashes a dark curve on pale cheeks. Her glorious black hair, in its usual long coil concealing her birthmark. Snuggled in a thick wrap, Melissa seemed asleep.

An allure too strong to fight, coaxed him forward, and in two strides he was beside her. Sinking onto the bench, he cupped her cheek and, stroking a thumb over her bottom lip, murmured her name.

"Melissa, wake up my love." The words out before he could stop them. She stirred, but did not open her eyes. His free hand sought hers.

He entwined their fingers and, leaning close, grazed his lips against her mouth. He felt her tremble, and waited. Her eyes fluttered open, a moonbeam catching their soft emerald radiance.

"Ged?" she muttered, and he heard confusion in her drowsy tones. "Are you really here, or am I dreaming?"

"I am here, see..." he lifted her hand to his heart, which was beating erratically.

"You're late." *Nicely done Melissa,* she grumbled inwardly. *He came through the maze to find you, and all you do is you complain. Wait ... he made it through the maze...?* "Why? No, not why are you late, why are you here, at the folly?"

He smiled then, a slow sensuous smile, drawing her gaze to his lips. *Oh Lordy*, she hungered for his kiss. Shuffling upright, Melissa tried to read his expression, difficult in the low light, while beneath her hand the beat of his heart quickened, and she heard his swift intake of breath.

"Tell me why you came through the maze," she repeated. The uncharacteristic tremor in her voice spoke volumes, and Ged threw caution to the winds.

"I love you, Melissa. I do not care about wagers or parents or subscriptions, or whisky or Randi. I believe I have loved you for some time, but my head did not grasp what my heart recognised weeks ago. I know this was not supposed to happen, but I want out of our wager. I wish to marry you, as soon as possible, not wait until the six months is up, and before you argue with me, I intend to kiss you."

His mouth on hers silenced Melissa's shocked squeak. Enfolding her in his arms, Ged's lips caressed, beguiled, and entranced. For a spilt second Melissa did not know what to do — her first kiss. Then she simply gave herself over to the incredible sensations his touch elicited.

Heat pooled in that most secret part of her, spiralling out along her veins. Without considering the consequences, she moulded herself to Ged. Her hands tracked up his chest, to curve around his neck, tangling into his shaggy hair.

His lips left hers, to trail a scorching path over her cheeks and along her throat. With one hand he lifted the thick twist of hair to scatter feather light kisses over her birthmark, nuzzling behind her ear.

"G-Ged... oh God, Ged!" Her head dropped back and she arched into him, the wrap falling away, exposing the satiny skin above the neckline of her gown.

With his lips and his hands, Ged wove a spell around her.

Melissa could not think, could scarcely breathe, but heavens, it was sublime. She unbuttoned Ged's riding coat, tugging his shirt from his breeches, desperate to touch him, hearing her name hiss over his lips when her chilled hands stroked his warm skin.

. . .

Her tentative gestures were delicious torture, and aware of how easily their ardour could consume them, Ged lifted his head, eyes dazed, and clothes awry. He stared at Melissa, similarly mussed, her lips slightly swollen, her expression dreamy.

"We must return to the house. Questions will be asked. Your reputation..."

Melissa placed a finger on his lips. "I love you, Gerard Mowbray. 'Tis the last thing I expected, but I rejoice in it. I do not give a fig for my reputation, all I care about it you. Forget convention and kiss me."

She drew his face close to hers, brushing her lips to his, her hands resuming their exploration — tempting, teasing.

"You are a minx, Melissa Bouchard," his breathing ragged under her torment.

"Hush..." sliding, until she lay full length on the bench, the cushion falling behind her head, Melissa's invitation was clear.

"Now," on a dramatic sigh, her nail grazing his skin as she trailed one finger all the way down his chest and over his stomach, to twitch at the waistband of his breeches. "I wager you are too fearful of flouting the rules, to demonstrate how much you love me."

Ged snorted with laughter. "Oh you do, do you?" She nodded, her eyes twinkling with mischief and something else — which set his heart, and most of the rest of him, on fire.

Gerard won.

EPILOGUE

ROME ~ SIX MONTHS LATER

*M*elissa was reclining on a small hillock in a sheltered corner of the Forum Romanum, under the ruined yet soaring colonnade of the temple of Castor and Pollux.

In front of her, two cows chewed contentedly on the grass. A few people, along with the odd horse and cart, meandered idly by — it seemed more a thoroughfare than an ancient monument, but Melissa was enraptured. Tilting back her straw bonnet, and turning her head slightly to the left, her gaze fell on Ged, who was sketching the scene.

They had been in Rome for three weeks, and this was their favourite place to watch the world go by. All manner of people, from lords and ladies, to merchants, to peasants, trod its grassy expanse. The weather was warm, the sky the brightest blue she had ever seen, and she was with Ged.

Uncaring of the dust gathering on her skirts, Melissa rolled onto her stomach, the better to study her husband. *Her husband*! She still struggled to believe they were wed.

The dream she presumed would remain elusive, had become her deliriously happy reality.

After their confessions at the folly — celebrated in a most satisfactory manner — the two made their dilatory way back to the house, pausing to share lingering kisses or a leisurely embrace.

Upon their return, neither seemed particularly perturbed their absence had been noted by *everyone*.

Two years passed her majority, Melissa did not require her father's permission to marry. Ged, however, with a mind to his reputation as a rake was determined to prove to Lord Shepparton that his intentions were sincere. Melissa's father declared himself delighted to bless Ged's suit, and the joyful nuptials were held a week after Christmastide.

Stunned at Ged's complete about face, Randolph Craythorpe cancelled the wager; relieved to have the freedom to court Felicity without worrying his friend would go all... well... Ged about it. He *was* moved to remark, that since Ged had finally fallen in love, there was a distinct possibility hell had frozen over.

They had been married for five blissful months and, currently, were in Rome. Melissa's other dream fulfilled.

Theirs was a fiery union — both were spirited, opinionated people — but they shared an underlying respect. It was rare their arguments lasted more than a few minutes anyway, because Ged simply kissed his wife into submission.

As though sensing Melissa's scrutiny, Ged twisted around to glance at his wife sprawled on the grass. Her chin rested on her hands, black curls tumbled out of the neat chignon with which she began the day, and her loosely tied wide-brimmed hat was perched on back of her hair at a rakish angle.

Their eyes met, and Melissa canted her head, smiling winsomely. Shifting onto her side, she crooked a finger and patted the grass.

"You have not kissed me for an age. I fear I shall not recognise your lips." She feigned a swoon.

"I'll wager I can remind you." He chuckled.

"Hmmm… your terms?"

Ged dropped his sketch, and swung around until he lay facing her. "These are my terms," his lips grazing hers. Anticipating her response, he waited, grinning.

Melissa tapped her chin, pretending to consider. "Oh I do beg your pardon, good sir, 'tis clear I propositioned the wrong man. My husband's kisses are far more… passionate."

She giggled at his expression, then lost her ability to function, when uncaring where they were, Ged crushed his lips to hers, kissing her until she thought she would burst into flames.

Undoing her bonnet, he tossed it towards their picnic basket, tangled his fingers through her hair, and continued kissing her senseless.

Melissa whimpered softly against his mouth, her hands flying over him, marvelling at the sensations running rampant through her.

Eventually, they broke apart, panting hard.

"Dash it all, Ged, you might let me win occasionally!" Melissa husked, trying to steady her breathing.

"I rather think you win every time, my love!"

"Well… I do relish a good wager."

EXCERPT FROM WINNING EMMA

SURRENDERED HEARTS - BOOK 3

"*M*arried? **Married**!" Randolph Craythorpe, Earl of Brackley, spat the words in fury. How the devil could she go from gentle flirting, and several dances an evening with him, to married? In the space of a fortnight no less. "Who is the lucky *gentleman*?" he gibed, his brain refusing to accept that Lady Felicity Hartwich, with whom he had shared more than one stolen kiss, and who seemed to return his affection, had upped and wed another, virtually under his nose.

"Timothy Archibald," Nathaniel Livingston, one of Randolph's two best friends replied.

"Westmoreland? That chinless wonder? Is this some kind of joke?" Timothy Archibald, the Duke of Westmoreland was a good fifteen years older than Randolph, and a man with little to attract a beautiful and much younger lady, except, of course, his wealth and his title.

"No joke, Randi. I believe it was an arrangement between him and the Hartwich family." Nathaniel watched his friend carefully. As a general rule, Randolph was easy going, and it took a lot to rile him up.

Unfortunately, when something tipped him over the edge, he forgot he was the first son of a marquis and tended to get roaring drunk which inevitably led to his behaviour deteriorating into the pugnacious.

"I need a drink"

"You do not, 'tis barely midday. What you need is a diversion." Nathaniel tapped his lips contemplatively. His wife, Juliette, mentioned her cousin would be arriving soon, from Bath, to spend the Christmas season with them.

Juliette was not a fan of said cousin, whom she considered selfish and conceited, but perhaps she might be the answer to an as yet unuttered prayer. "I have a suggestion." Randolph glared at him. "Hear me out." Going onto explain about the cousin.

"You want me to act as a babysitter for some silly debutante? That sounds like out of the frying pan and into the fire, Nate." Randolph was about to stomp off in high dudgeon when Nathaniel's next words gave him pause.

"It would make Lady Felicity jealous…" Nathaniel let that dangle, aware he was on thin ice. He had never met this cousin — she might have no looks of which to speak, but he was desperate enough to try anything.

Randolph had never shown any interest in courtship until he met Felicity, and the two had appeared smitten with each other.

Nathaniel frowned, in all honesty, he did not like Lady Felicity. She seemed… what was the word… detached, aloof maybe. In his opinion, not good enough for his friend, although he would never admit this to Randolph.

There were no rules when it came to love, those who claimed your heart often proved to be the most unsuitable — a hint of a smile tugging on his lips when he thought of Juliette.

What there *were* rules for was Society, and right now

Nathaniel needed Randolph to appear unmoved by the news that the woman he had fallen for had just married someone else.

About to reject Nate's proposal, Randolph heard the word 'jealous'. His lip curled in the parody of a grin and he found himself agreeing. If Felicity could treat him in so cavalier a manner, he was quite capable of returning the favour.

"Fine, but I reserve the right to renege on this agreement should she prove less homely than a church mouse."

Nathaniel hid a triumphant grin. Schooling his features, he inclined his head in grave acknowledgement, then invited Randolph to join Juliette and him for dinner that evening. It was easier to keep an eye on him that way!

Despite the best intentions of his friends, ten days and an outsize in headaches later, Randolph was still wallowing in self-pity. Juliette was no longer certain she wanted her cousin within a mile of the earl, his behaviour too immoderate even to be wished on so detested a relative.

The evening before the anticipated arrival of the guests, Nathaniel and Ged Mowbray, the third member of their group, took Randolph aside in the hopes of impressing upon him that being sober when introduced to Lady Charity was of paramount importance.

"Look at you," Ged scolded. "You look like a profligate rake and stink like a brothel. Why the major continues to trust you is beyond me." Referring to Major Withers, the man to whom all three were answerable.

"Because he knows I am the best." Randolph slurred, pointing a finger at his chest, his eyes bloodshot and bleary.

Nathaniel and Ged looked at each other, then back to Randolph.

"No help for it," Nathaniel remarked, meditatively.

"Only way," Ged agreed.

Each hooking an arm through one of Randolph's, they dragged him backwards down the slight slope to the bottom of the Livingston's garden.

"Sorry, Randi," Neither sounded particularly apologetic and, giving Randolph no chance to protest, dumped him bodily into the small pond. He landed with a loud splash, and for a few seconds was submerged completely.

There was a subdued roar when he reared up, shaking his head, water spraying everywhere. Saturated from head to foot, and in a towering rage, Randolph stood in the middle of the pond, which was only knee deep, and glared at his friends, so angry, words failed him.

"You reckon that did the trick?" Ged asked, studying his sodden friend dispassionately.

"Hope so, the fish couldn't take another dunking," Nathaniel replied with a chuckle, as the two turned their backs and strolled up to the house. Juliette met them on the terrace, arms folded, foot tapping,

"What did you do?"

"Randi will likely need to borrow some of my clothes." Nathaniel adroitly sidestepped his wife's question.

"Ged?" She pinned her gaze on his friend. Ged shrugged and raised his hands, palms up.

"He had it coming."

"'Tis the middle of winter, he'll catch his death. I am surprised the pond wasn't frozen."

"It might have been, but let's just say Randi was offering a service to the birds. They needed a drink."

"Oh, you…" Juliette's exasperation was easily mollified when Nathaniel dropped a kiss on her forehead.

"I apologise he has suffered a soaking, my love, but he needs to pull himself together. Charity arrives tomorrow, and if he has any chance of persuading Felicity her marriage has not affected him, he needs to have his head in the game, not buried in a vat of whisky."

While they were talking, another lady joined them. Tall, with a swathe of jet-black hair artfully styled over her face, Melissa Bouchard was Ged's very new betrothed. A state of affairs that shocked Society, as neither were considered marriageable.

Born with a twisted foot, and her lovely complexion marred by a purple birthmark which ran from the lobe of her right ear, across the edge of her cheek and halfway down her neck, Melissa had long believed she would never marry, for who would see past her flaws?

Gerard Mowbray simply did not see why he should be saddled with a wife when he could satisfy his urges without any commitment at all.

Recently, Melissa had proposed an intriguing wager, which seemed the answer to their prayers, but somewhere along the way, they realised the last thing either of them wanted had become their dearest wish.

"Randi always keeps things close to his chest. He appears to float through life without a care, absolutely unflappable. This business with Felicity has jerked him out of his customary complaisance. I have never seen him so ill-tempered." Melissa's thoughtful interjection prompted nods all round.

"We'll get him through this. He just needs to sober up. I thought I could hold my liquor, Randi could beat me into a cocked hat." Ged took Melissa's hand and drew her close. "Trust us."

"I always do," she murmured, resting her head against his shoulder for a heartbeat, before becoming her usual, practical self. "No time to dawdle. Come, Juliette, let us see whether our esteemed Lord Brackley might appreciate a towel and a hot drink. Mayhap our feminine concern will soothe his wrath."

Trying not to chortle at the bedraggled mess that was currently Randolph Craythorpe, Melissa made her way towards the pond, to offer what assistance she could, while Juliette rang for a maid to fetch a towel and lay out a set of fresh clothing in one of the guest rooms.

Thankfully, Randolph and Nathaniel were of similar build and once the former was dressed, they persuaded him to drink nothing stronger than hot chocolate for the rest of the evening.

ABOUT THE AUTHOR

Rosie Chapel lives in Perth, Australia with her hubby and three furkids. When not writing, she loves catching up with friends, burying herself in a book (or three), discovering the wonders of Western Australia, or — and the best — a quiet evening at home with her husband, enjoying a glass of wine and a movie.

Website http://rosiechapel.com/

A Christmas Prayer *with Ashlee Shades*

The Lady's Wager

Winning Emma

A Love Impossible

Unravelling Roana

Fairy Tale Romance

Chasing Bluebells

Contemporary Romances

Of Ruins and Romance

All At Once It's You

Cobweb Dreams

Just One Step

His Heart's Second Sigh

HISTORICAL FICTION

The Pomegranate Tree

Hannah's Heirloom - Book One

Hoping to trace the origins of an ancient ruby clasp, a gift from her long dead grandmother, Hannah Wilson travels to the fortress of Masada with her best friend, Max. Strange dreams concerning a rebel ambush begin to haunt Hannah and following a tragic accident. she slips into the world of Ancient Masada.

A woman out of time, Hannah must rely on her instincts and her knowledge of what will befall this citadel to survive. Will she escape, or is she doomed to die along with hundreds of others as Masada falls – and what does any of this have to do with an ancient ruby clasp?

Echoes of Stone and Fire

Hannah's Heirloom - Book Two

Pompeii - a vibrant city lost in time following the AD79 eruption of Vesuvius. Now rediscovered, archaeologists yearn for an opportunity to uncover the town's past. Some things, however, are best left alone - revealing the secrets hidden beneath the stones could prove perilous. Hannah and Max are brought to Pompeii by a surprise invitation to join an excavation team who are trying to uncover the city's long history.

After entering an excavated house that bears a Hebrew inscription, Hannah's two worlds collide, and she falls back through time to ancient Pompeii. A place where her ancestor is a physician to gladiators engaged in mortal combat, where riotous mobs run amok and where a ghost from the past returns to haunt her.

Will Hannah and her loved ones manage to escape the devastation she knows is coming, before the town is engulfed in volcanic ash?

Will she ever find her way back to Max the love of her life, waiting not so patiently millennia away? Or will echoes be all that remain?

Embers of Destiny

Hannah's Heirloom - Book Three

AD80 - Hannah and Maxentius must embark on a new journey to Northern Britannia. This harsh frontier is far from the comforts of Rome and danger lurks where least expected; a garrison of soldiers, some unhappy with their isolated posting; local tribes, outwardly accepting of their Roman occupier, but who may still resent the seizure of their lands.

Millennia away, Hannah Vallier finds a familiar item while working in a museum near Hadrian's Wall. It is the pomegranate; carved by Maxentius on Masada. Before Hannah can discuss it with Max, disaster strikes! Believing her husband has been killed, Hannah retreats into the past, her soul melding with that of her ancestor, but with little idea of what they could face. Is the risk from the conquered tribes, or much closer to home?

As rebellion threatens to shatter a fragile peace, Hannah's heart whispers that just maybe Max isn't dead and that he is calling her home. Can she trust her heart, or will she remain caught out of time, her destiny floating away like embers on a breeze?

Etched in Starlight

Hannah's Heirloom - Prequel

Maxentius - a Roman soldier fresh from the battlefields of Armenia, arrives to take command of the military outpost of Masada, Herod's isolated citadel in the Judaean desert. A seemingly mundane posting after years of warfare, Maxentius finds it more challenging to maintain a focused garrison than to face the wrath of the Parthians across a disputed frontier.

Hannah - a young Hebrew physician spends her days dealing with injuries from street brawls, deprivation, disease and loss. As her beloved Jerusalem plunges into chaos; her brother — who belongs to a band of rebels determined to drive out their Roman occupiers — tells her of their plans to storm a desert fortress and steal the weapons stored there, persuading his reluctant sister to go with him.

Masada - following the ambush, Hannah finds and treats three badly wounded Roman soldiers. In the aftermath and against impossible odds, Hannah and Maxentius realise that they are more than healer and captive, their fate already etched in starlight.

Prelude to Fate

For Lucia, staring into the jaws of an horrific death, escape seems impossible.

Rufius Atellus, a veteran Roman soldier, is appalled when he recognises one of the victims about to be executed. Surely this is a ghastly mistake?

A ferocious she-wolf, anticipating a tasty meal, suddenly finds herself under a human's control.

In an unexpected twist, and as danger threatens, the lives of all three become inextricably entwined.

Was it chance brought them together in that theatre of bloodshed, or simply a prelude to fate?

REGENCY ROMANCES

Once Upon An Earl

Linen and Lace - Book One

When Fate saw fit to intervene in the life of Giles Trevallier, the very
respectable Earl of Winchester, by dropping a female — soaked to
the skin and with no memory of who she is or how she came to be
there — literally at his feet, no one could have predicted the
outcome.

While uncovering her identity, Giles realises he is falling hopelessly
in love with his mystery guest, who unbeknownst to him, is
succumbing to similar emotions; but, when the heart is involved, a
thoughtless word or gesture can thwart even Fate's best-laid plans.

Faced with misunderstandings, whispers of scandal, secret
documents and foreign agents, their chance at a happy ever after
seems elusive, but fairy tales often happen when least expected, and
love — however inconvenient — usually finds a way to conquer all.

To Unlock Her Heart

Linen and Lace - Book Two

Abused by a duke, and shunned by Society, relief seems at hand
when Grace Aldeburgh is bequeathed a house in a small village, far
from malicious gossips.

Once there, a tentative friendship blooms between Grace and Theo
Elliott, the local doctor, who has already resolved to be the man to
unlock her heart.

Just when happiness appears to be within her grasp, her erstwhile
tormentor once again stalks Grace. After a failed kidnap attempt,
the duke's quest culminates in an acrimonious confrontation, and
the reason for his venal pursuit becomes agonisingly clear.

Love on a Winter's Tide

Linen and Lace - Book Three

Every day, Helena disappears into a world few acknowledge, helping the poor, downtrodden, and abused. A husband is the last thing she can be bothered with.

Busy managing his shipping line, Hugh Drummond sees no need for a wife, whose only joy is dancing and frivolity. If — and it was a huge if — he ever married, it would be to a woman as capable as he, not some giddy society Miss.

Then, Hugh meets Helena and despite their resolve, fate, it seems, has other ideas. As their attraction deepens however, treachery threatens to tear them apart. Will they uncover the perpetrator in time, or will their love be swept away, lost forever on a winter's tide?

A Love Unquenchable

Linen and Lace - Book Four

Jessica Drummond, a bright and cheerful young woman, rarely gives romance, let alone love, a thought. Long hours working in her brother's shipping office affords little chance of her ever meeting an eligible bachelor.

Duncan Barrington, veteran of the Napoleonic Wars, believes himself wounded in both body and soul. He has no intention of inflicting his demons on anyone, certainly not a beautiful and, in his opinion, irresponsible city lady.

One cold and snowy morning, the plight of a bedraggled puppy throws Jessica and Duncan together and, as a spark of something indefinable yet wholly unquenchable begins to burn, it is unclear who rescued whom.

A Hidden Rose

Linen and Lace - Book Five

After witnessing his mother's grief at the loss of his father, Nick

Drummond resolved never to cause someone he loved such distress. Even the happiness of his siblings would not sway him – until he met Rose.

Rose Archer was almost content assisting her doctor father in a tiny fishing village in the north of Yorkshire. To experience the world beyond, a tantalising dream – until she met Nick.

Unexpectedly, the impossible becomes possible, and the renounced – desired above all things, but the shipwreck that brought them together, may yet tear them apart. Will Nick learn to trust his heart, or will his love for Rose remain forever hidden

The Daffodil Garden

A Regency Romance

Horrifically scarred during the war, William Harcourt - Marquis of Blackthorne - prefers to spend his days in the quiet of his daffodil garden; plants do not pity, turn away, or judge.

Lucy Truscott, whose life is far removed from that of the *ton*, has no idea that by saving the life of a young woman, to whom she bears an uncanny resemblance, her own will be placed in mortal danger.

A chance encounter leads to something more. William begins to trust that Lucy sees the man beneath the scars, while Lucy is persuaded that love might actually transcend status.

Unfortunately, before their courtship has really begun, someone has every intention of ending it - permanently.

The Unconventional Duchess

Refusing to suffer the humiliation of her husband flaunting his mistress at Society events, the newly married Duchess of

Wallingstead, Ella Lennox, takes control of her life. She leaves London for the family's country seat in remote Yorkshire.

A woman alone, Ella spends the next four years turning a cold, grim house into a home, and transforming the fortunes of the estate. Not afraid of hard work, she soon earns the respect of those around her with her determination and unconventional attitude.

Out of the blue, the duke arrives. Resigned to another arduous visit, Ella is stunned when it seems he is attempting to court her.

Impossible!

Could her dream of a happy marriage be about to come true?

Everything hangs on a snowstorm, a herd of cows and an uninvited guest!

Rescuing Her Knight

The de Wiltons - Book One

A story, invented to keep a little girl distracted, marks the beginning of another tale. One destined to remain unfinished for nearly twenty years.

Against her better judgement, Kitty de Wilton is persuaded to help Adam Marchmain banish his demons. This requires a subterfuge which, if discovered, might shatter more than the bonds of friendship forged two decades previously.

To Kitty, determined to break through the shield Adam has erected, the risk is worth it.

To see his smile and hear his laughter.

To rescue the knight of her childhood.

Just when a fairy tale ending is within her grasp, Kitty is threatened by the man who murdered her husband. In a cruel twist the tables are turned, and Kitty is the one who needs rescuing.

His Fiery Hoyden

A Novella

Livvy has no respect for the nobility; they let her down when she most needed them. Why should she accede to their demands now?

Philip, Lord Harrington, is stunned to discover the young heir to the dukedom lives a stone's throw away in a ramshackle cottage, and resolves to restore the child to his birthright.

They meet in a clash of wills, but just when it seems Livvy might surrender, the victory Philip desires, may not taste all that sweet.

A Regency Duet

Luck be a Pirate

Luck wasn't something retired pirate Kennet Alexson believed in – good or bad. However, even he had to concede that landing a job at Trentams shipyard, and meeting Lynette Collins, was more than coincidence.

Fortune it seemed, was smiling on him for once.

As Kennet adjusts to life on dry land, his friendship with Lynette deepens into something far more enduring, and what once seemed elusive now becomes possible.

Unfortunately, fate has other plans, and Kennet's good luck is about to run out.

The Highwayman's Kiss

Surrendered Hearts – Book One

Nothing exciting had ever happened to Juliette St Clair. Her days were spent assisting her father or calling on friends, wandering art galleries, taking constitutionals or, and more preferably, escaping into her books. Her evenings her evenings — an endless round of balls, where she preferred to remain invisible.

Until the day she was robbed by a highwayman.

A Regency Christmas Double

Heart Rescued

Four years since Jasper lost the woman he was hoping to marry. Four years since he closed his heart and withdrew from Society. He has no idea his reclusive existence is about to be shattered.

Enter his sister's best friend, Harriet, a flame haired beauty, who needs his help.

Reluctantly he agrees and as they spend time together, it is clear their feelings run deep. Although Harriet affects Jasper in a way no woman ever has, he believes her to be out of his league ~ but it's Christmas and she might just be the one to melt his frozen heart

Catch a Snowflake

Romance often blossoms in the most unlikely of places - but in a ward full of wounded soldiers - surely not?

When Lucas Withers comes face to face with Jemima Parsons - a young woman who blames him for her brother's injury - falling in love is the last thing on their minds. What neither of them anticipated, was the magic of snowflakes.

Fate is Curious

A Novella

Happily, ever after? No such thing! Bereft, following her beloved husband's sudden death, Lady Charlotte Sherbrooke has lost her belief in such romantic nonsense.

Successful shipping merchant, Zacharie Romain, is no stranger to loss; his business can be hazardous. Moreover, his wife died in childbirth and even though it happened a decade ago, he has no mind to expose himself to such sorrow again.

They meet in less than joyful circumstances but, as the year turns and grief diminishes, the woes of a small boy become the catalyst for something wholly unexpected. Can Charlotte and Zacharie trust what Fate has in store or will past heartbreak prevent them from taking a chance on love?

A Christmas Prayer

with Ashlee Shades

A Short Story

An entreaty from a frightened child.

Orphaned and only nine, Caroline Thorne has to grow up before her time. She is doing everything she can to keep what is left of her family together and out of the workhouse but is terrified her prayers are not being heard. Or maybe they are...

A petition from a woman desperate for a family.

A chance meeting with three orphaned siblings, tugs at Elizabeth Barrington's heart strings. Thus far, she and her husband have not been blessed with children and, as Christmas approaches, a plan begins to form - one which might just be the answer to her prayers.

Two Christmas prayers, as different as they are the same.

Will they hear and, more importantly, heed the answer?

The Lady's Wager

Surrendered Hearts- Book Two

A Novelette

Ged Mowbray will do anything to avoid being married off to the suitable prospects his parents insist on parading in front of him.

Melissa Bouchard is under no illusion her sizeable dowry is the attraction to suitors, not her.

An overheard conversation leads to an offer too good to refuse, but what happens when a lady's wager, becomes a gamble on the happily ever after, you did not even realise you wanted?

Winning Emma

Surrendered Hearts - Book Three

A Novelette

Randolph Craythorpe — earl, covert operative, and occasional highwayman — believed his dalliance with Lady Felicity Hartwich would lead to marriage. It did, but not to him! The arrival of an unwelcome guest, however, provides the perfect opportunity to indulge in a little retaliation.

Emma Newbury accompanies her cousin, Lady Charity Anscombe, to London for the Christmas season. Once there, she comes face to face with the three men who witnessed the humiliating aftermath of her father's disgrace — one of whom, to her irritation, has taken up residence in her dreams.

Their infrequent encounters only serve to confuse but, while winter tightens its grip on the city, what was inconceivable becomes the one thing for which they both yearn, yet bound by Society's rules, cannot admit.

As the snow falls, Randolph begins to understand that to win Emma, he will have to surrender.

A Love Impossible

A Regency M/M Novelette

Tasked with investigating a heinous crime, Edward Lindsay travels from London to Dublin — a city which holds too many memories — in the guise of guardian to his sister. He knew it could be hazardous, and relished the challenge, but that wasn't what caused his stomach to tighten as they approached landfall.

Dublin held more than just a murderer.

There was also Aidan.

While attending a party, Aidan Griffen is astonished when he comes face to face with a man who fled Dublin two years previously. A man he has desperately tried to forget.

As Edward closes in on his quarry, a fire, deliberately extinguished, is rekindled. But what of it? Edward and Aidan share a love impossible, and to acknowledge their feelings — more dangerous than confronting a killer.

Is there any hope of a happily ever after?

Unravelling Roana

A Novelette

Tired of being ignored by her husband, Roana Dumont, Countess of Brooketon does the one thing guaranteed to get his attention. She runs away... to Venice, leaving behind a set of riddles for him to solve... *if* he feels their marriage is worth saving.

Gideon Dumont, 6th Earl of Brooketon is flabbergasted when he discovers his wife has apparently vanished off the face of the earth. A series of puzzles, the only clue as to her whereabouts.

The question is... will he unravel them?

FAIRY TALE ROMANCE

Chasing Bluebells

A Novella

Once upon a time, somewhere in France, there was a man whose reckless obsession led him down a dark path. One which, ultimately, cost him his life.

That ought to have been the end of it. Regrettably, as is so often the case, those who least deserve it, suffer for the actions of others.

A decade after being sent away, Sebastien Daviau returns to the little village where everything began, hoping to lay the ghosts of his childhood to rest, studiously ignoring the possibility, he might run into Charlotte de Montbeliard.

As luck would have it, Charlotte is the one who runs into him… well his horse. Although the encounter leaves a lasting impression, neither recognises the other.

A name revealed causes a freak accident, catapulting Sebastien's past into his present, and bringing him face to face with a man whose reputation would intimidate the most ardent of suitors.

Can whatever is blossoming between Charlotte and Sebastien survive the challenge imposed, or is their happily ever after about to fade as quickly as the bluebells they loved to chase?

Of Ruins and Romance

While escorting a group of tourists around the ancient Roman port of Ostia, Kassandra Winters bumps into someone she first met in less than auspicious circumstances two years previously. The encounter leads to a job offer - to be the assistant guide for a three-week tour of ancient sites in and around Rome. Unable to resist such an opportunity, Kassie agrees.

Kassie has intrigued Gabriel St Germain since he accidentally knocked her flying outside her university professor's office. Her face haunts his dreams, yet he never expected to see her again. So, he is surprised when she appears, as though destined to do so, in the middle of a ruin, and he concocts a plan to win her heart.

Gabriel's old-fashioned courtship touches something deep inside Kassie and, although struggling to believe someone as handsome as Gabriel could possibly be interested in her, she soon realises she has fallen irrevocably in love with him.

However, just as Kassie shares everything of herself with Gabriel, her world comes crashing down. Can their romance survive, or will it fall in ruins, like the relics of antiquity that brought them together?

All At Once It's You

When Alex arrives in the small village of Rosedale Abbey, to take up a position as a research assistant for a renowned archaeologist, the last thing she is looking for, or expects to find, is love.

Jake was perfectly happy with the status quo. When it came to relationships, he didn't do committed or long term. He called the shots, and if his current flame didn't like it, she knew what to do. A philosophy, which served him well - until he met Alex.

Romance blooms, but even as the untamed wilderness of the North Yorkshire moors weaves its spell, a long-buried secret might yet jeopardise their happily ever after.

Cobweb Dreams

A Contemporary Novella

A holiday on the Scottish isle of Mull was just the break Chloe Shepherd needed, an escape from her boring office job and her complete lack of anything resembling a social life. Romance, it seems, isn't on the cards and, although Chloe dreams of finding her soulmate she is beginning to believe love is like cobwebs — spun overnight, only to vanish in the early morning breeze.

Under sufferance, Dominic Winters makes a flying visit to Mull to check on a rental property owned by his family. He hasn't got time for this — so indulging in a holiday fling is the last thing on his mind.

A lamb stuck in a bog proves a most unexpected matchmaker and, while Mull weaves its magic, Chloe wonders whether those fragile cobwebs might be far more stubborn than she thought.

Just One Step

A Short Story

In the aftermath of an horrific car accident, Daisy Forrester travels to Italy - hoping, so far from her memories, she might begin to heal.

Archaeologist, and single father, Adam Willoughby is too busy looking after his young daughter to give romance let alone love, a thought.

Neither expects a chance encounter in an ancient ruin to be anything more, but sometimes, that's all it takes.

His Heart's Second Sigh

A Novella

Reuben Faulkner and Paige Latimer are two happily single people, who have no desire to upset the status quo.

Unexpectedly, they are thrown together, only to discover both want far more than a casual friendship.

Just when things take an interesting turn, Reuben's past catches up with them, and threatens to derail their blossoming romance before it has chance to start.